This Book Belongs to...

_____

_____

_____

ME!

Not My Hats

An original concept by author Tracy Gunaratnam

© Tracy Gunaratnam

Illustrated by Alea Marley

First Published in the UK in 2018 by

MAVERICK ARTS PUBLISHING LTD

Studio 11, City Business Centre, 6 Brighton Road,
Horsham, West Sussex, RH13 5BB
© Maverick Arts Publishing Limited 2018
+44 (0)1403 256941

American edition published in 2021 by Maverick Arts Publishing,
distributed in the United States and Canada by Lerner Publishing
Group Inc., 241 First Avenue North, Minneapolis, MN 55401 USA

ISBN 978-1-84886-707-9

Maverick
publishing

distributed by **Lerner**

Not MY Hats

Written by
Tracy Gunaratnam

Illustrated by
Alea Marley

Hettie **loved** hats: **tall** hats, small hats, **any size** at all hats, round hats, **pointy** hats, **fancy hoity toity** hats.

And Hettie wore them **all**.

One day, Hettie was fishing in her usual spot on the ice when up popped Puffin.

"I need a **hat**," he said.

Hettie opened her bag, "I'll share my **bunny**, my **dollies**, my **slippers** and my **lollies**, my **books** if you wish, and I'll even share my **fish**...

...but I'll **never, ever** share my HATS," she said.

Suddenly, Puffin felt hungry and he forgot all about the hats.

"I'll take the fish," he said, and off he went.

Hettie put down her fishing rod.

It's time to change my hat, she thought.

She tried lace hats,

space hats, some in your face hats,

mop hats, flop hats, even over the top hats and she was just about to make her decision when...

"I need a hat," said Puffin.

Hettie shook her head. "Listen, Puffin," she said.

"I'll share my bunny, my dollies, my slippers and my lollies, my books if you wish. and you know I share my fish, but

I'll never, ever share my HATS!"

Suddenly, Puffin's feet felt cold and he forgot all about the hats.

"I'll take the slippers," he said, and off he went.

Fishing can be boring and Hettie closed her eyes;

soon she was floating through **the hatmosphere.**

I've never seen so many hats, she thought.

There were...

...pirate hats, jester hats, pork pie and sou'wester hats,

cork hats, crown hats, witches and clown hats.

Then...

"**Wake up**," said Puffin,

"I need a hat."

Hettie growled, "I... don't... share... **hats!**"

"How about swapsies then?" asked Puffin, and he opened his backpack. "I'll swap... a **gnome**?"

"No!"

"A comb?"

"NO!"

"A dog with a bone?"

"NO!"

"A fig?" "A twig?"

"No!" **"No!"**

"A pot-bellied pig?"

"No!"

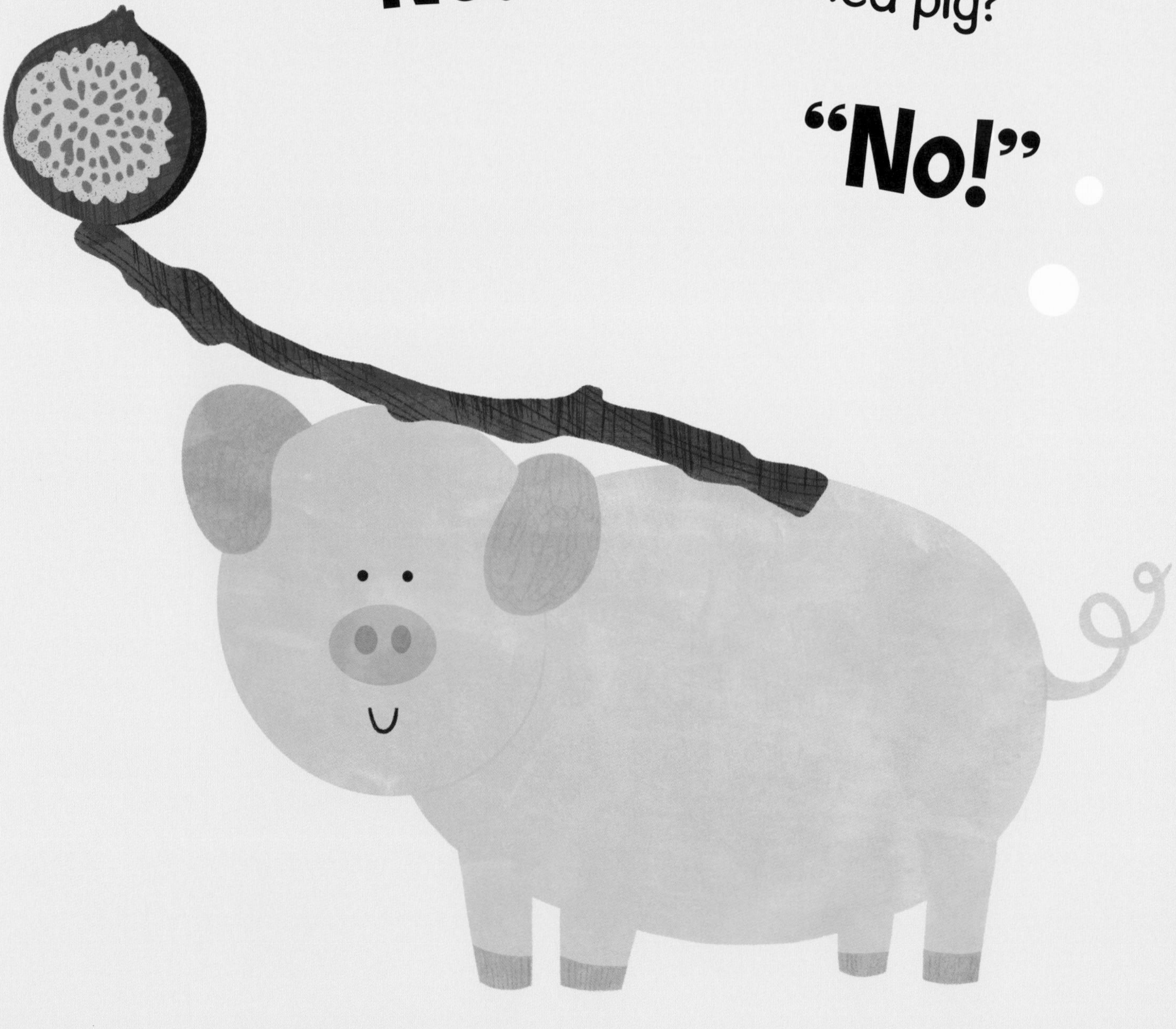

"**Yes!**" said Hettie,

"I need a scarf! Scarves look **splendid** with hats."

"And hats look **super** with scarves,"

said Puffin. Hettie had a thought...

"Sharing my hats might not be **so** bad. Here,"

she said, and handed Puffin the **handsomest** of hats.

Puffin was delighted.

"I've got plenty of scarves," he said.

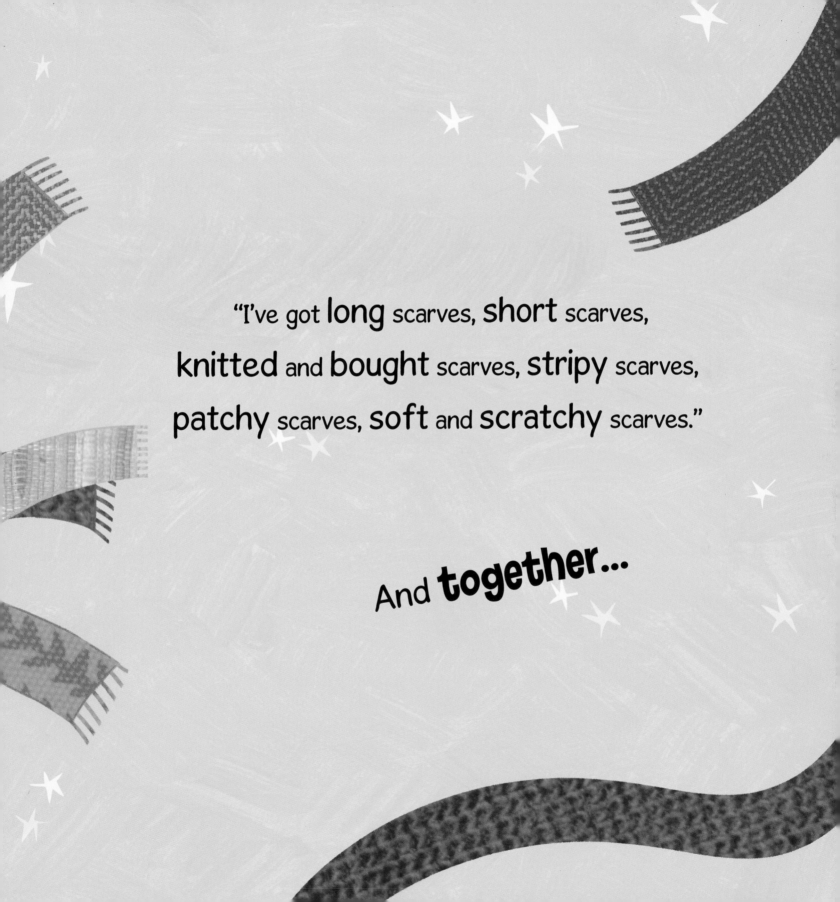

"I've got **long** scarves, **short** scarves, **knitted** and **bought** scarves, **stripy** scarves, **patchy** scarves, **soft** and **scratchy** scarves."

And **together**...

...they wore them all.

The End

E CAR
Carle, Eric
The very lonely firefly

071812